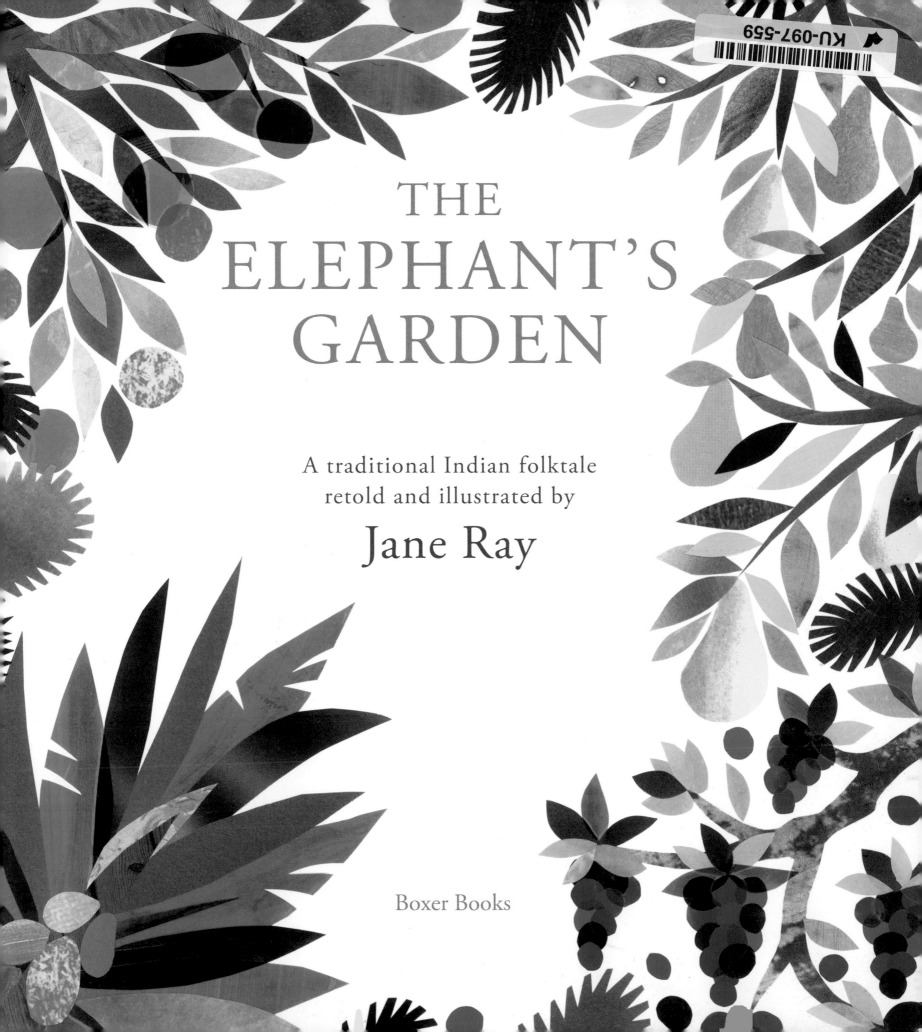

THE ELEPHANT'S GARDEN

A traditional Indian folktale
retold and illustrated by

Jane Ray

Boxer Books

In Jasmine's garden there grew the most delicious fruit in the whole village.

There were apples and apricots,
kiwis and kumquats,
papayas, peaches
and passion fruit.

But every night, something was eating the very best fruit.

"Well, we can't have this!"
thought Jasmine.

One night, when everybody else
was in bed, she climbed out of
her window and hid behind the
lotus tree. The hours passed.
The moon rose.

Jasmine kept watch.

CRASH!

An elephant fell from the sky!
He munched all the mangos.
He guzzled all the grapes.
He chomped all the cherries.

"Stop right there, Mr Elephant!" shouted Jasmine.
"You've eaten all our fruit!"
"I'm very sorry, but I was hungry,"
said the elephant. "And the fruit
here is so delicious. Come with
me and let me show you
my garden."

Jasmine grabbed the
elephant's tail and they
took off over the treetops.
They flew past the moon.
They flew past the stars.

They landed on a cloud where another garden grew.

Everything in this garden was . . .

ENORMOUS!

The peaches were as big as footballs
and the oranges were the size of ostrich eggs.

The elephant gave Jasmine a gigantic plum. But it was as hard as glass and impossible to eat. Every fruit looked delicious, but was really a precious jewel. "No wonder you prefer the fruit in my garden," said Jasmine.

At sunset the elephant was hungry again.
He offered Jasmine one ruby strawberry to
show her mum, and they flew back home.

Jasmine's family were very worried
about her. But they could hardly
believe it when she showed them
the great big ruby strawberry and told
them about the elephant's garden.
They wanted to see it for themselves.

"I'll take you tonight," promised Jasmine, "but you mustn't tell anyone or they'll all want to come."

But Little Hassan saw his friend Kali.
"It can't hurt to tell Kali,"
thought Hassan. "After all,
she is my best friend . . ."

Who told Aunty Sita and Uncle Deepak.
Before long everybody had heard
about the precious jewels in
the elephant's garden.

Kali went straight home and told her mum. Who told her cousin Bakool.

"If we can have some of those jewels for ourselves we will be rich!" they said.

When the moon rose, there they all were,
wanting to visit the elephant's garden.
They hid in the bushes and waited, until –

CRASH –

the elephant landed by the mango tree.

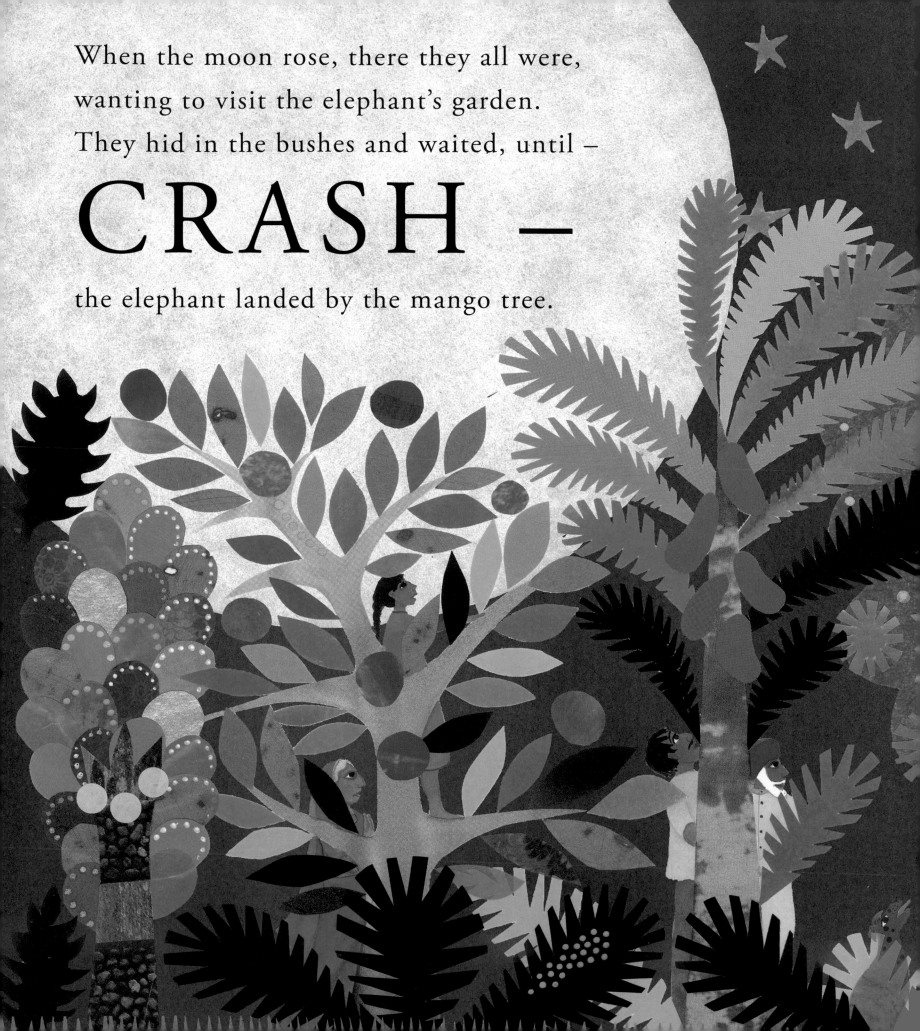

But Cousin Bakool couldn't wait.
"Tell us now," he said.
"They are as big as ostrich eggs," said Jasmine.
Cousin Bakool had never seen an ostrich egg.
"How big is that?" he called up from the
bottom of the line.
Exasperated, Jasmine shouted,
"They are this big!" and she held
out both her hands . . .

And she and Little Hassan, Kali and Aunty
Sita, Cousin Bakool and all the other friends
and relations, tumbled back down to earth
and landed with a wallop by the mango tree.

The elephant never came back.
He must have found somewhere
more peaceful to eat his dinner.

So Jasmine's family and friends
never did visit the elephant's
garden after all.
But they did get to eat the
delectable dates and plump
apricots, the sweet strawberries
and luscious lychees in
Jasmine's beautiful garden.

For Maureen Hanscomb
Jane Ray

First published in Great Britain in 2017
This paperback edition first published in Great Britain in 2021
by Boxer Books Limited.
www.boxerbooks.com

Text and illustrations copyright © 2017 Jane Ray

The right of Jane Ray to be identified as the author and
illustrator of this work has been asserted by her
in accordance with the Copyright, Designs and Patents Act, 1988.

The illustrations were prepared using cut-paper collage and paint.

The text is set in Adobe Garamond Pro

ISBN 978-1-910716-62-5

1 3 5 7 9 10 8 6 4 2

Printed in China

All of our papers are sourced from managed forests and renewable resources.

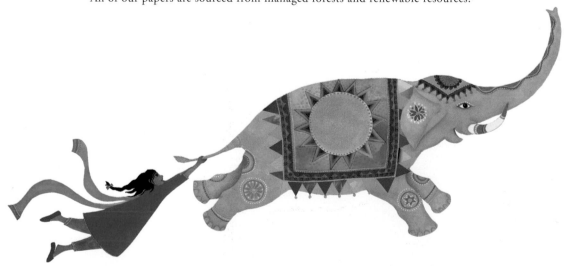

DISCOVER MORE BOXER BOOKS TITLES

Three magical and enchanting anthologies, which include some of the best-loved stories of all time.

 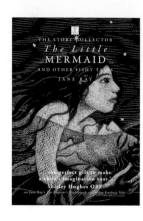 

The Emperor's Nightingale and Other Feathery Tales   **The Little Mermaid and Other Fishy Tales**   **The Lion & The Unicorn and Other Hairy Tales**

Praise for these wonderful gift books:

"Only an author and artist of Jane Ray's dazzling talent could do justice to this stunning collection of bird stories, which she has told with elegant simplicity and illustrated in full colour throughout. This is the perfect gift to make a child's imagination soar."
– Shirley Hughes OBE

". . . stunning illustrations . . . this is a wonderful collection to share . . ."
– Julia Eccleshare, Love Reading and the Guardian children's book editor

"A book to be relished for its text, art and overall design."
– Booklist

". . . visually stunning . . . a gorgeous collection."
– School Library Journal

BIG BOB,
Little Bob

James Howe

illustrated by Laura Ellen Anderson

WALKER BOOKS
AND SUBSIDIARIES

LONDON • BOSTON • SYDNEY • AUCKLAND

When **Big Bob** moved in next door, Little Bob's mother said, "Isn't that nice! You will have someone new to play with. He even has the same name as you!"

To Little Bob, their name was the only
thing about them that was the same.
For one thing, Big Bob was big.
And Little Bob was, well, little.

But how big or how little they were didn't matter to Little Bob. What mattered was what they liked to *do*.

"Boys do not play with dolls," said
Big Bob. "They play with trucks."

"I do not like trucks," said Little Bob. "They are too noisy."

One day, when Little Bob was teaching his students their letters…

"I'm sorry," Big Bob said. "You were supposed to catch the ball."
"I'm not very good at catching," said Little Bob.
"Then you can throw and I'll catch," Big Bob said.

Little Bob shook his head.
"I'm not very good at throwing either."

No matter what they did, Big Bob and Little Bob did not do it the same.

Then one morning,
a new girl moved
into the neighbourhood.

"Why are you playing with dolls?" the girl asked.

"Um," said Little Bob.

"Huh!" The girl snorted. "Didn't anybody ever tell you that boys do *not* play with dolls?"

"Hey! You stop picking on my friend!" Big Bob told the girl. "Boys can do whatever they want!"

The girl put her head down and turned away. "Wait!" Little Bob said. "What's your name?"

"Blossom," the girl said. "I just moved in next door."
"Do you want to play with us?" Little Bob asked.

"Okay," said Blossom. "But I like playing with trucks more than dolls."

"That's all right," said Big Bob. "Girls can do whatever they want, too."

The three friends played together from that day on.

Big Bob ... Little Bob ... and Blossom.